# Steamy Creek

*A Cozy Romance Anthology*

Jan-Carol
Publishing, Inc
*"every story needs a book"*

Steamy Creek
A Cozy Romance Anthology

Published January 2024
Mountain Girl Press
Imprint of Jan-Carol Publishing, Inc.
Copyright © 2024 Jan-Carol Publishing, Inc.
Front Cover Design: Tara Sizemore
Cover Photo: © CleverStock/Adobe Stock

ISBN: 978-1-962561-18-1
Library of Congress Control Number: 2024932203

Jan-Carol Publishing, Inc.
PO Box 701
Johnson City, TN 37605
publisher@jancarolpublishing.com
www.jancarolpublishing.com

*To the authors who helped make this anthology a reality and to every reader unable to resist the allure of* STEAMY CREEK.

# Table of Contents

# Steamy Creek

# The Fishing Hole

## Delonda Anderson

Marlon stood in the kitchen with his arms crossed, fit to be tied. The only thing that ever seemed to quell his anger was fishing. He crammed together a couple of cheese sandwiches, snuck in an extra piece of light bread, and tossed them in a sack. He sauntered into his room and eyed his nightstand. A crisp ten-dollar bill and eight shiny new quarters glimmered at him and mocked him, like a chump. He'd worked all that summer bailing hay. And for what? That money was supposed to buy her something pretty. His brows furrowed and he stood there for a moment sucking the air between his teeth. He picked up a quarter and dropped it in his pants pocket, then walked outside to his father's shed and grabbed his fishing rod and old tackle box. He made his way onto the old country trail toward Lucky's Grocery.

Old men, with their dog-tired overalls and jaws bubbled with tobacco, were already gathered underneath the front awning at Lucky's, talking politics, Germany, and a looming war. Some men sat adjacent to the store on old stumps and metal lawn chairs, gab-

1

bing or watching a mean game of checkers. As Marlon made his way toward the steps, one of the old men yelled,

"Afternoon, Marlon. Looks like you're goin' fishing."

"Yessir," Marlon replied.

"Oughta try that little shade piece on Vinsant Lake," another man offered. "I hear tell they's a mess of shad in them waters."

"Reckon I might," Marlon said, passing the store threshold.

He picked out a chocolate bar and clapped down his quarter at the register.

"You okay today, Marlon?" asked Mrs. Fairborne.

"I'm right fine, thank ye," he answered.

"You look awful peek-ed."

Marlon put his head down and his face reddened. Mrs. Fairborne shook her head as she rang up the candy and gave him back twenty cents change. He stowed the candy bar inside his lunch sack and hurried outside to the pop machine. He slid a nickel in the slot, opened the glass door, and pulled out a nice, cold bottle of Co-cola. He downed the drink, bought another for lunch, and made his way toward the lake.

On the far end of Vinsant Lake was a bank where trees hung across the edge and shadowed a good portion of the water. Slight breezes congregated gently among the cattails there, and the shade beckoned animals of all kinds to rest and cool off from the roasting summer sun. That's where Marlon headed. As he circled the perimeter, he stopped, sudden and rigid. He wasn't alone. Elaine Goode sat on the bank's edge dressed in her brother's tattered overalls, swinging her bare legs, and holding a long fishing pole over the water.

Marlon's shoulders sank. His grip on the tackle box gave way and hit the ground with a *thunk*. He pursed his lips and grabbed it again, looking askew at Elaine, who didn't seem to notice. He closed his eyes and sighed a little, then straightened upright. He strolled toward the perfect spot, about a yard or two away from the girl, and emptied his gear. He reached inside the sack for a bit of bread, jammed it in his pocket, and walked a few paces toward her.

"Where's your sister?" he asked, lightly kicking at a stump. He took the bread out of his pocket and smashed it between his fingers.

She shrugged then answered, "Janet's at home."

Marlon stepped to his spot and grabbed his rod and reel.

"How come?" he asked, piercing the dough onto the fish hook.

Elaine cocked her head to the side and looked up at him, her eyes squinting from the sun. She smiled.

Marlon's eyes shot open with that flicker of green-eyed understanding. "Is that Johnson boy up there courtin' her?" Marlon asked.

Elaine nodded. Marlon's whole body tensed. He clenched his jaw and his face flushed hotter than the devil.

"He was talking to Daddy when I left," stated Elaine.

"Talkin' to—"

He stopped mid-sentence and glared daggers at her. At that moment, she became all the problems of the world. The more he glared, the more he saw himself in her reaction. She'd stopped swinging her legs. Her eyes tinged with a mixture of fear and pity and something else he couldn't quite discern. Water welled in them and her lips forced a tiny, quivering smile. She was downright nerve-wracking. His gaze softened a little. A fish plopped out of the water and reminded him why he was there in the first place. That made him madder at the girl than anything. She disrupted his peace, his thinking time. He swiftly went back to his spot and settled in.

"What're *you* doin' here?" he asked.

"I figured you'd be here," she said, looking across the lake. She raised her eyebrows and flattened her lips, and never took her gaze

3

from the water. "Came here to make you a bet."

"A bet?"

"Yep. That I can catch a bigger fish than you can."

Marlon scoffed. "That right?" he asked with a little grin.

"Heard how you got a knack for fishin'—that you catch big fish."

With sweeping gestures, she drew up her line and grasped the little chicken bone tied to the end. Elaine dug in a bucket, yanked out a worm, and fixed it to the bone. Marlon's eyes fixed on her delicate hand and the wriggling little creature. He looked down at his own morsels of bread, then back at the bucket.

"You got *nightcrawlers?*" he asked.

"Been digging 'em up here and yonder about a week."

Marlon pulled in his line and edged closer to Elaine. He cleared his throat. "You got the best spot anyway," he said.

"Always have," she said.

Marlon patted his pockets. "Cain't find my bread," he lied.

Elaine casually pulled up the bucket and plopped it down between them. Inside were all kinds of worms—and not just nightcrawlers, either. His face reddened. He'd been working so hard bailing hay that summer and was plumb tuckered out by the end of the day. Nightcrawlers and worms were the furthest thing on his mind. But there they were in that bucket, squirming like sin, and caught by a girl.

"Take you one," she offered.

"You sure your brother didn't ketch these?"

"Carl don't like worms. Says they give you a disease," she said. "Take one if you want, or don't take one. Don't matter squat to me."

"'Ppreciate it," he said as he skewered a fat one on the hook.

He looked at her pole and line. Elaine had cast just a short distance. He snuck a peek at her, his eyes askance, and snickered. He zipped back his rod and cast hard and far. He knew where the big fish were. *Way* out there.

"You mind me being here," she asked, "instead of—"

Suddenly, Elaine's line grew taut and she gripped the pole as it tugged her forward. Marlon jumped up, his eyes wide and beaming.

"Pull it in, Elaine!"

Elaine stood, dug in her heels, and moved up the bank. She pulled and pulled with her pint-sized strength, but whatever was on the line jerked her forward. Marlon hurried over and reached for the line.

"NO!" she yelled. "*I'm* gonna win the bet."

Marlon chuckled, then stood akimbo with his arms crossed. "Gotta do a better job than that. Probably a little bluegill wrasslin' you in."

"You'll see," she said, grinding her teeth.

She pulled harder, but the force dragged her down the bank and into the water. She still held her grip. Marlon smacked his knee and had himself a good guffaw. Elaine drew the pole closer to her, grabbed the line, and hauled it up. A fish, big as the world, flopped at the end. She grappled with the it, hooked her finger in its mouth, and walked out of the water a muddy mess.

Marlon's mouth opened wide.

"That's the biggest shad I ever seen!" he exclaimed.

Elaine dragged the fish up the bank. Her mud-splotched face glowed in the hot sun. "Do I win?" she asked with a wide-eyed grin.

Marlon wrinkled his brow. "Never said I'd do it," he muttered. He sat down, picked up his own rod, and looked across the water.

Elaine's shoulders slumped. Her lips flattened, her mouth drew downward, and her light green eyes stung through Marlon like a hornet in a hen house.

"I figured," she said, stomping forward. She took her catch and secured it on a rope at the shallow end of the lake. She stomped back, plopped down, and grabbed the pole.

Marlon shook his head. "Never seen a girl catch a fish that big."

"I ain't a'talkin' to you," Elaine seethed.

"What did *I* do?" he asked, surprised.

"You don't notice things...people," she said. She grabbed a few twigs, pulled back her long, brown hair, and secured it into a knot. She grabbed another worm, attached it to her line, and cast hard. "Don't notice what's good for you...*who's* good for you."

Marlon slowly turned his head and looked at her—really looked at her. He never noticed before how pretty she was. He always thought she was just some kid who taunted him for fun. She was no more than fourteen. He was about to turn seventeen in a month. She looked a hot mess. Bits of hair escaped the knot and dangled down her face in a mad nest sort of way. Mud had already splotched and caked on her face. Her overalls were wet and her feet looked like she wore dirt for shoes. But, to Marlon, these things made her even prettier. No, he thought, there was something *real* about her.

She turned and fixed her gaze on him. Her pretty eyes were teary and entreating. A realization hit him like an arrow to a bullseye. He knew then. He knew all about this day and why she came. Here. At this lake. Under this shade. Before he knew it, he blurted, "They's a barn dance on Saturday."

Elaine sniffed and turned her gaze ahead. "Yeah," she murmured.

"You wanna go?" he asked.

She laughed. Laughed like she was putting one over on the devil. Marlon sank. Something in the pit of his stomach knotted up and made him queasy. He told himself he ought to stay away from them Goode girls. His face was on fire.

6

"What's so damn funny?" he asked, scornfully.

"That was my bet!"

"What?"

"My bet was if I catch a bigger fish than you do, you have to take me to the dance."

He sat there, perplexed and dumbfounded—at her, at fate, at how life can be lousy one minute, then beautiful the next. He twisted around to face her and caught his breath. Sunlight shimmered through the trees and a gentle wind sent the leaves into a flutter. The light twinkled across her skin. Even from her profile, she beamed. He cleared his throat and faced the lake.

"Starts at seven o'clock," he stated.

"Mmhmm," she replied. "Daddy already said I can go 'cause the barn belongs to old Farmer Watkins." Her legs see-sawed back and forth, then she stared at him, her eyes full of mischief. She continued, "Then he said to me, 'Remember Lainey—pretty is as pretty does.'"

Marlon's cheeks flushed and his eyes searched the ground. He spied his lunch sack and grabbed it, then pulled out the two cheese sandwiches and cola.

"Here," he said. "I made two a'these. You want one?"

"Well, I am a little hungry," she answered. "Thanks."

He scooted a little closer to her. She retrieved something wrapped in a kerchief, and carefully opened it. His eyes widened. Two bread biscuits slathered to the heavens with blackberry jam.

"Helped Mama make 'em myself," she said.

He took a bottle opener from his tackle box and shared the cola. They picnicked underneath the shade, laughing and talking. Suddenly, visions of Elaine in all her pretty Sunday dresses flashed in his mind. One dress in particular rested there.

7

"What're you gonna wear?" he asked.

"Mmmm. I was thinking," she said, pulling at a piece of grass, "I was thinkin' I might wear my little green dress. Matches my eyes, you know."

Marlon's face beamed with a big, wide grin. "I'll come by your house at 6:30," he said, "and walk you there...if that's okay with you."

"Why, don't you know it is?" she asked.

# Emily's Consequence

*Karen Bruce*

## EMILY

"Are we there yet?"

Emily looked in the rearview mirror and gave her son, Henry, the evil eye. "If you ask me that one more time, I'm going to drop you off at the next rest stop." Feeling just a teensy bit guilty for telling her son a blatant lie, Emily took a deep breath and said, "Judging by the way my sinuses are acting up, it won't be long."

It had been a while since they had been to visit Emily's mother. There were so many reasons not to go to Bristol. The first being that Henry was not a good traveler. Henry had the patience of a gnat, a very annoying gnat. Another reason was the fact that every time Emily came home, her allergies became unbearable. She knew she should have taken her allergy meds the night before, but she forgot. Another reason was the biggest of all the reasons, and it scared her to death. She just prayed that she didn't run into him, even though his dad

9

lived next door to her mother.

Emily's mother had called a couple of days ago begging for her help. She had tripped on the uneven sidewalk in front of her house and broken her femur. Since Emily and Henry were out on break for the summer, she didn't have an excuse not to go, and her mother wasn't able to travel to her house in North Carolina. She lived in a condo with steps and her mother complained about them even when she was walking properly.

"I'm starving."

Emily sighed. "Your grammy said she had all kinds of food at her house from her neighbors and friends. I'm sure you'll find something to eat as soon as we get there."

"You know I'm picky. We don't know these people and what kind of hygiene habits they have."

Henry had a point there, and he was definitely a picky eater. "Okay. The exit is another couple of miles."

Emily's stomach began to tense just thinking about being back in Bristol. She had come in on occasion but never stayed very long. There were too many memories of the little house she had grown up in. She had lived there all her life and Luke lived next door. Luke. She tried not to think of him, but the closer she got to home, the more the memories came flooding back. The night that Henry was conceived was the most beautiful night of her life, but the next morning was the worst. Luke told her it had been a mistake and he was sorry. Later, when she realized she was pregnant, she made up her mind that even though Luke didn't want her, she wanted his baby.

Looking back, she wasn't sure how she graduated with a teaching degree while raising a baby, but she did. Her mom and dad helped her a lot, but Emily was determined one way or another, with or without their help. The only person who knew that Luke was Henry's father was her mother. She made her mother promise not to tell anyone, especially Luke.

Emily had loved Luke her whole life. They grew up together. Their mothers were best friends, so they were more like siblings. Emily's feelings changed when they were teenagers, but Luke always treated her more like a sister, until she came home for Christmas break during her freshman year of college. Luke was broody and depressed because his mother had been diagnosed with cancer. Trying to cheer him up, Emily had taken him to see the Christmas lights at the racetrack. Instead of making him happy, it only made him more depressed because it may have been his mother's last Christmas. Emily was heartbroken for Luke and did the only thing she could think of. She held him and told him it was going to be okay. She stroked his hair and then his shoulders, and then it happened. He turned to her, not as a friend, but in the way she had dreamed of for so long. It was desperate and intense and so spectacular that she could never forget it. Henry was conceived in love; at least for her part, it was love. Luke was just using her, apparently, and regretted it. He regretted it as soon as it happened, which was a real blow to her heart and her ego. Coming back and confronting Luke for any reason just wasn't possible. She was still mad at him, but she also felt guilty for never telling him he had a son.

His mother held on for a couple of years before she died. Emily's father had also died from prostate cancer when Henry was about five years old. He loved his Papa more than anything. Emily hated cancer. Why did it seem as if everyone was getting cancer?

After getting fast food, Emily turned into the old neighborhood. The oak trees were getting way too big and causing all of the sidewalks to buckle and crack. No wonder her mom had tripped. Emily and Luke had walked on those sidewalks for many years to and from their elementary school, which was maybe a half mile from their homes. It had been a wonderful childhood, so carefree and fun. There was no internet or cell phones. They played outside every day.

Emily pulled her small SUV into her mom's driveway and tried not to look next door. She focused on getting her son and anything else she could grab quickly and headed towards the house before anyone noticed her. She would get the rest of her luggage later, preferably when it was dark. Henry beat her to the door and tried to open it, but it was locked. Emily rang the doorbell and then remembered she had a key. She began rummaging through her pocketbook while Henry danced around.

"Hurry, Mom! I gotta go!"

Just as she finally found the key, she heard some rustling on the other side of the door and then it slowly opened. Her poor mom looked awful. "I'm so sorry, sweetie. I thought I had unlocked it, but I guess I didn't."

Emily pulled the storm door open so Henry could go in. He hollered as he sprinted past his grandmother, "Sorry, Grams, I'm in a hurry."

Betsy was holding on to her walker and still wearing her nightgown. Emily knew she must be in bad shape if she still hadn't changed her clothes. Betsy was very meticulous about her appearance and usually had every hair in place.

"I got here as fast as I could. How are you feeling now?" Earlier that morning, Betsy had told Emily that she was in a lot of pain, but it was bearable.

"I'm okay. The doctor said I'm doing well and that the worst is over. It's almost time for my pain pill." She walked to her recliner and slowly sat down. "This electric recliner is wonderful but it's so dadgum slow. If the house was on fire, I'd be a cooked goose."

Emily stood next to her mom. "What can I get you?"

"Nothing right now. Just sit down and let me look at you."

About the time Emily sat down on the couch, Henry came running back in. "Grammy! Mom said you broke your leg! Can I see it?"

"Henry! Don't be rude."

"Don't you fuss at him." Betsy turned to Henry. "It's in a cast, sweetie. It wasn't a bad break, thank goodness, but it cracked enough to be a nuisance. Grammy's getting old and her bones aren't what they used to be."

While Henry asked her mother twenty questions, Emily got up and went to the bathroom herself. Her mom had hired someone to update the bathrooms and kitchen and it was Emily's first time seeing the results. It wasn't fancy, but it was updated and modern. Emily liked the blue-gray walls and splashes of green in the decorations. She washed her hands and walked back to the living room. Henry had already made his way into the kitchen.

"Henry is looking for the cookies I bought him. He's still hungry."

"He's always hungry these days." Emily looked perplexed. "Did you go to the store?"

"No. I ordered some groceries online and had them delivered." Betsy smiled. "Can you believe it?"

Emily laughed. "I have to admit, I'm a little surprised."

Betsy lowered her voice. "I just want to warn you that Luke moved back to Bristol."

Emily's heart sank. He had been living in the neighboring town, Johnson City, for a few years. After graduating from ETSU, he decided to live there. He started his own used-car business and had done really well, according to her mother.

"Why?" Emily whispered.

"His father said that he and his girlfriend broke up. He sold his car lot and is going to open one up over here." Betsy picked up her water bottle and took a drink. "He's actually living with his dad until the house he bought is ready. He closes in a few weeks."

Emily hung her head and pressed her temples with her fingertips. "This is not good, Mom."

Betsy looked sheepish. "I know and I'm so sorry. I would have never asked you to come, but I was desperate." She leaned back in her chair and closed her eyes as if in pain. "I had nobody else to ask."

Looking at her mom, Emily felt guilty. Her mom had always been there for her, so she had to suck it up. Hopefully Luke would be so busy that he wouldn't even notice Emily's car in her mom's driveway.

Later that evening, Emily helped her mom wash up and get a clean gown on. Once she was in bed, Emily began straightening up the bathroom and kitchen. After checking on her mom once more, Emily grabbed her water bottle and joined Henry, who was in the backyard kicking his soccer ball around.

Henry was such a great kid. She couldn't have asked for a better son. When he was about five, he began asking about his father. At first, she was vague about Luke, but Henry wouldn't let up, so she lied and told him that his father had died in an accident. She hated herself for lying about it but felt she had no alternative. She even lied about his name when Henry had been insistent about knowing it. She said his father's name was Brian. She had even made up all kinds of stories about how heroic Brian was because it seemed to make Henry so happy.

Emily watched Henry as he tried to kick the ball and keep it from touching the ground. He was so athletic and reminded her so much of Luke when he was that age. He had dark hair like Emily, but he had Luke's bright, blue eyes. Luke's hair was blond and would turn almost white every summer. Emily was lost in her own memories and didn't hear Luke come into the backyard until he was almost in front of her. Her mouth hung open in shock.

"Well, if it isn't little Emmy." Luke stood there smiling, having no clue of the turmoil that raged inside her head. "Dad said you were coming to help with your mom. I'm so sorry she broke her leg."

Emily could only nod because the capability of speech had left her. She knew it would be hard to see Luke, but she underestimated how hard it would actually be. It was impossible, and she was acting like a ninny.

Henry came over and held his ball to his side. Just seeing him knocked some sense into her. "Hey, Luke."

"Who is this?

Emily looked at Henry and wondered if she could lie about her son but in the end finally blurted, "This is my son, Henry."

Luke held out his hand. "Nice to meet you, Henry. I'm Luke. I've known your mom all my life."

Henry shook Luke's hand and Emily just stared. They had different coloring, but it was so obvious to her that they were father and son. Emily panicked. Would everyone else know? What was she going to do? For years, she had been able to keep them apart and then her mom broke her stupid leg!

Henry looked a little perplexed about his mom but spoke to Luke in a mature way, just as she had taught him. "Nice to meet you, too. Do you play soccer?"

Luke laughed. "Yeah, I play a little soccer. I can't right now but I promise while you're here we'll kick the ball around a little. Sound good?"

Henry nodded exuberantly. "That would be awesome!"

15

Luke turned back to Emily and grinned. "It was great seeing you again, Emily. Give your mom my love."

Emily could only nod her head and say, "Sure."

Only after he left could she breathe. Trying not to let her son see the uproar in her brain, Emily turned and grabbed the broom leaning against the house and began sweeping anxiously.

## LUKE

Luke couldn't believe it when his father told him that Emily was coming home to help Betsy. Maybe now he could talk to her and get some closure. Things went from bad to worse when they were together that Christmas after his mom had gotten her cancer diagnosis. He overstepped and let things get out of hand. It's not that he didn't want to be with Emily, but she had always been like a sister to him and then all of a sudden, things changed. He was mortified that he took advantage of her and tried to explain but instead of making it better, he made it a hundred times worse.

He tried to call her, but he knew from the tone of her voice that things had changed, and they could never go back. The problem was that he couldn't get her out of his mind and knew that what they had shared was special. He compared every girl he was with to Emily, and nobody else came close. She was the only person in the whole world who knew him completely and didn't judge him. And then he ruined it. His mind went through a million different ways he could have handled it better.

He thought maybe now they could talk, but when he walked over and saw her in the backyard with her son, he knew right away that he still loved her. He loved her as a friend but also much more than that. Just looking at her face automatically made him smile and remember the good times. She was his voice of reason when he was being hot-headed. She was the calm that brought him back down. She was the one he turned to when he was upset or happy. She was the one he went to for everything. Losing her had been as profound as losing his own mother.

When she saw him and their eyes met, it was the old Emily, but then he saw her whole demeanor change. He didn't know what he had to do to make it better, but he would do whatever it took. Henry, her son, was a surprise. Luke knew he had been her first but apparently not her last. She had gotten pregnant at school, and he had been so devastated. He had expected to feel resentful of her son, but it was the opposite. The kid was amazing, he could tell right away, but what did he expect with a mother like Emily?

## EMILY

"Mom!"

Henry ran into the house at breakneck speed shouting at the top of his lungs. Emily and Betsy were both startled and instantly alert. The house was warmer than Emily was used to and every time she sat down to read or relax, she felt her eyes drifting close. Henry's excitement woke her up and got her adrenaline pumping.

"What in the world? Are you okay?"

"Luke wants me to go down to the school and play some soccer. He said they had a pretty good field down there. Can I go? Please?"

Emily looked at her mom in that 'told you so' sort of look. Betsy shrugged her shoulders and didn't look offended at all. Emily's first instinct was to say 'no,' but Henry would be crushed judging by the

17

look of excitement on his face. "Okay, but be careful."

Henry didn't reply but ran out of the house as fast as he ran in it.

"See! I knew this would happen!"

At first, Betsy was silent. She picked at some object on her pants and looked like she was about to burst but wouldn't speak up.

"What? Just say it."

Betsy sat up a little straighter. "Well, don't you think it's time, Emmy?" She had that knowing look that mothers have. "The more time goes on the harder it will be, and Luke has every right to know that he has a son."

Emily hung her head. Tears came unbidden to her eyes. She fought it but they just kept coming. She had cried too many tears over the years, and she was tired of it. She was tired of hiding it from Henry. She was tired of pretending and lying and everything that comes with keeping a secret for almost nine years.

So quietly she almost didn't hear herself, Emily whispered, "I know."

Betsy sat in silence and let her daughter work it out for herself. She gave her time to construe that her revelation would cause havoc and heartbreak, but ultimately it would also give her relief, which she needed more than she had realized.

Again, she said, "I know," with more conviction this time. Emily stood up and began pacing. "Oh, Mom, how am I going to do this? Henry and Luke are both going to hate me."

Betsy took a drink of her diet soda as if talking about secrets of this magnitude happened every day. "They'll be mad at first, of course, but as time goes on, it will get easier, and they'll forgive you."

Emily rolled her eyes and looked up. "Oh, God, please help me!"

## LUKE

Luke watched Henry run and kick the ball, and the more he watched, the more he wondered. He reminded him of someone. They were both hot and sweaty and decided to take a water break. Luke praised him and told him what a great job he was doing and that he would definitely be scoring some goals next season. He said, "How old are you?"

"I'll be eight on my birthday, August 18."

"You definitely didn't get the short genes from your mother."

They both laughed. Henry said, "Yeah, my dad, Brian, was tall."

"Brian?"

"Yeah, he was a pilot in the Air Force and his plane went down. He was a hero."

Luke looked puzzled. "The Air Force? What was his last name?"

Henry closed the cap on his water bottle and put it on the bench. "Fleenor. He had the same last name as Mom. They weren't related."

Luke nodded. He knew something wasn't right. All of a sudden everything came together. He knew. He knew with certainty who Henry was, and his whole world changed in an instant.

## EMILY

Emily had been pacing the whole time Henry and Luke had been playing soccer. She had to tell Luke the truth, but how? Her mom was no help because the pain pill she had taken earlier made her sleepy. She dozed while Emily fretted and tried to come up with a plan to make it easier on everyone, but she came up with nothing.

As soon as Henry walked in the door with Luke behind him, she knew all her plans would have come to naught anyway, because judging by the look on their faces they already knew.

She closed her eyes and hung her head in shame.

## BETSY

Betsy had been trying to think of some way to get Emily back home ever since Luke had moved back to Bristol. She knew if she didn't do something drastic, Emily would never get up the courage to tell the truth. When she tripped on the sidewalk and broke her leg, she knew it was the perfect scenario.

Understandably, Luke and Henry were mad at first, but sooner rather than later they all came to a place of forgiveness. Betsy's leg had healed, and she was getting ready for the wedding that would soon take place. Her daughter and grandson had moved back to Bristol, and they would soon get their *happily ever after*. Sometimes mamas had to intervene on their children's behalf. She just wished her best friend, Lisa, Luke's mother, could be here to share it with her.

Betsy looked up. "We did it, Lisa. We finally got our wish."

# Her Knight in Flannel Armor

*Susan Dickenson*

Madison balanced precariously on the top step of her stepladder as she reached up to cover yet another splotch of paint on the crown molding in her parlor.

"I should have painted the ceiling before the crown molding," she said in frustration.

"Perhaps if you had taped off the molding with painter's tape you would've painted a cleaner line," offered a male voice from the front screen door.

Startled, Madison dropped her paintbrush and braced herself against the wall to keep from falling off the stepladder. She steadied herself and climbed down.

"Don't you know not to sneak up on someone when they're on a ladder?" she accused.

"I'm sorry, I didn't mean to startle you. Though, I did knock," he said. "I heard you were looking for a painter, so I came over—"

"I didn't hear a knock." Madison picked up a rag and walked toward the doorway, wiping paint from her hands. "As for needing a painter, I need one very badly because I'm *lousy* at painting."

He ran his hand through his hair and grinned. "I can see that." The lovely woman grimacing before him had spatters of charcoal gray paint on her hair and face. "Are you always this cordial?"

"What? Oh, I'm sorry," Madison apologized. "It's just that I recently moved here and can't seem to get anything done with this house." She opened the screen door and motioned for him to come in. "But if you could start painting right away, I can get the house in some sort of order before my family descends upon me," she added as she walked to a makeshift workbench and retrieved a clean paintbrush.

He frowned as Madison handed the brush to him. "Paint?"

"Yeah—you said that's why you're here." His hesitation at taking the brush gave her pause to notice what a tall, cool drink of water he was, even if he was just wearing jeans and a flannel shirt. She felt her face flush. "Um, I'm sorry. I don't know where my manners are. I'm Madison, and you are?"

He smiled. "Tucker. Nice to meet you, Madison." He motioned toward the ladder. "You could use a taller ladder."

"If I had a taller ladder, I wouldn't have bungled the painting so badly. I tried to use tape, but I couldn't reach high enough to get the tape on straight. Well, if that hotel owner hadn't hired all the painters in town, I wouldn't need to paint this myself."

"Hmm," Tucker said. He crossed the room and climbed up the stepladder. "'Descend' doesn't sound very positive. When will your family arrive?" he asked as he began to touch up the molding.

"I guess I shouldn't have put it that way, but Mom didn't really want me to move so far away from home." Madison picked up a scraper and began removing loose paint from a windowsill. "They'll be here in three weeks, not nearly enough time to get this house presentable," she sighed. "At least not for Mom. This house isn't exactly her taste."

"It does need a lot of work, but I've always thought this was one of the most beautiful Victorians in town."

Madison nodded in agreement. "I fell in love with it the minute I walked through the front door. It was as if I had found my home. Do you know much about architecture, Tucker?"

A knock at the door interrupted the conversation. "Now that knock I heard," Madison chuckled. She walked over to the screen door. "Can I help you?"

An older man in overalls stood there wringing his hat in his hands. "I'm looking for Mr. Mallory, miss. Is he still here?"

"Mallory?" she stammered. "As in The Mallory Resort Hotel?"

"Yes, miss. His mother sent me over to fetch him."

"It's okay, Mr. Howard," Tucker said as he came up behind Madison. "Just tell Mother I'll be along shortly."

"Well, alright then. Good day, miss," he said as he placed his hat on his head and turned to leave.

Madison looked at Tucker in disbelief. "You're Tucker Mallory? Why on earth are you here painting my parlor?"

"My mother decided to change the entire color scheme of the hotel before the spring season begins," he grinned sheepishly. "When I heard you were asking around for a painter, I decided to come here and apologize for tying up all the painters in town." His shoulders instinctively shrugged as his eyes surveyed the room. "After I got here and saw the state of *your* painting, well, I thought the fairest thing to do would be to help you."

Madison looked at the handsome man in front of her with splotches of paint on his shirt and laughed. "I guess pleasing our mothers isn't always easy."

Tucker reached out and brushed a paint chip off her chin. "No," he said. His sheepish expression transformed into a warm, intense gaze. "But I have a feeling spending time with you will be. Shall we?" he asked, gesturing with his paintbrush.

For a moment, Madison could not find her voice. Tucker's deep tone and sensual charm disarmed her completely. "By all means," she stammered. "I'm certainly in no position to turn down the offer."

Tucker smiled and simply returned to the stepladder to finish the crown molding. Madison resumed the task of scraping paint from the windowsill. *I wonder if I should offer to cook him dinner?* she thought. A quick glance at Tucker provided the answer. *Most definitely, but only* after *Mother leaves.*

\* \* \*

Madison looked around her parlor for one final inspection in anticipation of her mother's arrival. The clean paint lines looked very nice—mostly due to Tucker's help. He had painstakingly completed the touch-up work on the crown molding and had even helped her finish the windowsills.

"Everything look okay?" she heard Tucker say from the screen door.

"Tucker?" Madison said as she spun toward the door. "What are you doing here?"

With a sheepish grin, he raised his hand and gently waved a bottle of wine. "I thought I might drop off a bottle of our latest vintage of Blueberry Fields and a cheesecake for you and your mom."

Madison opened the screen door for him. "That's very thoughtful," she said. "But she's due any minute."

"Exactly," he said simply as he headed for the kitchen.

Madison and Tucker had been enjoying a great deal of each other's company since they met. She had changed her mind about waiting until her mother left to cook for him. She prepared shrimp scampi for him that first evening and he invited her to the hotel for dinner the next. Cooking for each other became somewhat of a routine. She had even met his mother—who reminded Madison of her own mother. Olivia Mallory seemed to be the force behind the Mallory family business and was a no-nonsense type of woman. She didn't suffer fools, as the saying goes, which rivaled Madison's mother's temperament.

Madison followed Tucker to the kitchen. "I thought we had decided I would ease Mom into the idea of me *dating* before you met her," she groaned.

"And that's still the plan," he replied. "I'll only be a moment, just long enough to put these things in your fridge. You're not expecting her for another hour, right?"

"That would be incorrect, young man."

Madison's heart skipped a beat as her eyes met Tucker's. The expression on his face resembled what a thief getting caught in the middle of a jewel heist might look like. Madison grimaced but quickly replaced that with a smile.

"Mother, you're early," she said as she turned around. "How was your trip?" she asked as she went to hug her mom.

Her mother returned the embrace. "Traffic was fine, Madison," she replied. "But I'm more interested in discussing who this young man is," she remarked as she released Madison.

Tucker closed the refrigerator door and held out his hand in greeting. "Please allow me to apologize, Mrs. Quinn. My name is Tucker, and I didn't mean to intrude on your visit with Madison."

Mrs. Quinn raised her eyebrows and directed an all-too-familiar expression of combined accusation and impatience at Madison.

"Mother, this is Tucker Mallory. He's..."

"Your *boyfriend*, I presume," Mrs. Quinn interrupted.

Madison was incredulous. "Boyfriend is a little high-schoolish, Mother," she hastily replied.

"Oh?" her mother remarked. "Then that description fits right in with you running away."

"I didn't run away from anything, Mother," Madison protested. "I'm allowed to live my own life and follow my own path." Madison glanced at Tucker. "I'm sorry, Tucker, would you mind?"

"Not at all," he said. "We'll speak tomorrow?"

"I'll call you after while," she whispered as she hugged him good-bye.

Madison waited until Tucker left before confronting her mother. "I've never been more embarrassed. Do you have to behave like that?"

"I don't appreciate your tone, Madison. I'll thank you not to be disrespectful," she admonished.

"Mother, you walked into my home unannounced and embarrassed me in front of Tucker. I think the disrespect is coming from you."

"Does he know you ran away from your fiancé?" Mrs. Quinn accused.

"I did not and do not have a fiancé," Madison replied firmly. "Whatever you and Spencer and Spencer's parents had planned was just that—your plans."

"You dated all through high school and college, Madison. Our families have celebrated holidays and milestones together for years," she replied. "You know it's expected that you marry Spencer."

"I cannot be held to what you and Spencer's parents expect. Let me rephrase that, I will not be held to anyone's expectations," Madison asserted.

26

"I don't know what's gotten into you, but I can see you have been sorely influenced by that young man!"

"Tucker has absolutely nothing to do with my decisions. I left because I didn't want my life mapped out for me by anyone other than myself. If you think you can come here and tell me how to live my life, you may as well go home now."

"I came here to take you home, Madison."

"I am home, Mom."

"We'll see about that, but for now I'm going to the hotel," Mrs. Quinn retorted.

"The Mallory Resort Hotel, I presume?" Madison said sarcastically.

"Yes, why?" Mrs. Quinn replied.

"That's Tucker's family's hotel and I'll thank you not to embarrass me any further."

\* \* \*

"Are you alright?" Tucker asked Madison as he poured her a glass of wine.

"Okay, I guess," she sighed. "I'm so sorry about my mom. She means well enough, but she considers herself the matriarch of the family and thinks she has to orchestrate everything and everyone."

Tucker poured a glass for himself and sat beside Madison on the settee in her parlor. "Sounds familiar," he chuckled. "I didn't realize your mother had booked into the hotel. I would've made sure she had a room facing the lake."

"I'm sure she's fine," she replied wearily. "Thank you for coming back over, Tucker."

"Happy to oblige and even happier to enjoy this cheesecake with you," he smiled. "Ready for a slice?"

27

Madison giggled. "Cheesecake makes everything better?"

"Most certainly, well, that and a glass of blueberry wine," Tucker added with a wink.

* * *

Madison awoke the next morning feeling nervous and somewhat worried. She had a lot to think about. She hadn't expected her mother to be so angry about Tucker. *What did I think was going to happen*, she thought. *Mother still expects me to marry Spencer!* She shrugged and turned on the shower faucet. She would just have to hope her mother was in a better mood this morning so Madison could explain again why she left.

Madison was showered, dressed, and drinking coffee at her breakfast table when the doorbell rang. She groaned, carefully set her coffee mug on the table, and went to face the harridan that she knew must certainly be grimacing on the other side of her front door.

"Mother," she said absentmindedly as she opened the door. "I hope you..." Madison stopped mid-sentence as she realized who was standing in front of her. *Spencer!* she thought wildly.

"Maddie," Spencer said simply as he opened the screen door. "You look wonderful." He leaned in to kiss her cheek, but she put her hand up and pushed him further onto the porch. The screen door closed behind her.

"What are you doing here, Spencer?" she demanded.

"Maddie, I know you wanted to make a point about your *freedom*, but it's time to come home. We have a wedding to plan."

"So, it's true then, you're engaged to be married?" Tucker said from the front walkway.

"Tucker," Madison grimaced.

"Yes, we are engaged," Spencer replied smugly.

28

"No, we most certainly are not!" Madison fumed. "Spencer, you need to leave. Now!"

Tucker wasn't sure what to do, but the mortification displayed on Madison's face stirred his protective instincts. He quickly closed the distance between them and scowled at Spencer. "I think you were told to leave," he advised.

"Who do you think you are?" Spencer challenged.

"My *boyfriend*," Madison emphasized.

"You're in a relationship?" Spencer accused.

"Didn't Mother tell you? She was introduced to Tucker last night," Madison said a little more gleefully than she should.

Spencer did not respond but simply stomped across the porch and down the steps to the walkway. He turned around and opened his mouth as if to say something, but spun back and marched to his car. His tires barked on the pavement as he sped off.

Tucker grinned at the sheepish expression on Madison's face. "Boyfriend?" he asked.

"You're a friend, who happens to be a boy," she shrugged.

Tucker moved closer to her and put his hands on her waist. He looked at her longingly, his eyes dark and sultry.

"And that's all?" he asked softly.

The huskiness in his voice sent butterflies through her. She reached up and ran a finger across his lips. "Would you care to step into my parlor, Mr. Mallory?" she purred.

"As long as you don't bite, Ms. Quinn," he teased. His lips formed into a devilish grin. "Or maybe even if you do."

Madison moved her hand to the back of Tucker's neck and pulled him closer.

"I won't make any promises," she breathed as his lips grazed hers. She reached behind her and opened the door with one hand while

29

pulling him inside with the other.

Madison's foot caught the doormat, causing her to stumble slightly. Tucker swiftly caught her and scooped her up into his arms.

"That's the second time I've almost fallen in front of you," she laughed.

"Just think of me as your knight in flannel armor, my lady," he said as he carried her across the room.

Madison kissed his neck. "Sir Mallory has a good ring to it," she teased.

"I think Lady Mallory sounds even better."

His proclamation caused her breath to catch. "Are you asking me..." she said hesitantly, allowing the words to taper off.

Tucker put her down and took both of her hands in his.

"To be my lady?" he finished for her. "Madison, I know it's a little sudden, but yes, I'm asking you to be my wife."

Madison's eyes became misty with tears. *I came here to find my freedom and a home, but it just may be that Tucker is what I was looking for all along,* she thought.

"I've always wanted a Christmas wedding," she replied.

"As in eight months from now?" he chuckled.

"Can we manage it?" she asked.

Tucker laughed. "With my mother and yours? Not a problem—and we already have the venue, if the hotel is okay with you?"

"With all the freshly painted walls? I think your mother must be psychic," she giggled.

"That's something to ponder," he said. "I might never have met you if she hadn't demanded that we change the décor."

"I'll thank her next time I see her," she said as she placed her hand in his. "But for now, Sir Mallory, my parlor awaits."

# A Tender Kiss

*Susan Noe Harmon*

Joe Asher stood in front of the old homeplace for one last time. It had been several years since he had placed a foot on the property near Johnson City, Tennessee. After his parents' death, he and his wife tried to live in the hundred-year-old house, but the repairs seemed to drain his wallet faster than he imagined. The wildlife was plenty up in Asher Holler but not the human kind. His wife was never happy living in a remote area with the closest neighbor being two miles away. After one huge argument, he decided to close up the house and move to Virginia where his in-laws lived to make his wife happy.

After Sally died, Joe still wore his wedding ring. He felt it was more of an obligation. He watched as his wife of many years succumbed to cancer. No children were born of their union, which caused an underlying tension within the household. Unfortunately, Joe was unable to give her a child due to his time in the military, having been exposed to toxic chemicals during a special ops mission in Desert Storm.

Avoiding splintered wood on the rotting steps, Joe moved his feet carefully on the creaking porch, reaching the front door without falling through. Unlocking the door with the antique skeleton key, he entered the world of his past, his childhood, and the memories of family life in the mountains. Sunbeams showed through the dirty windows, giving enough light to see the old furniture his mother kept clean and polished every Saturday no matter whether company was expected or not. Now, the air felt musty and dank; it was a sense of emptiness.

He peeked inside each of the five rooms, choosing not to enter. There was no reason. *I've made my decision and now all I need to do is collect any family heirlooms I want to keep,* he thought. *I need to check the attic. I remember Mom stored boxes of stuff up there for years.*

He pulled down the attic door, turned on his flashlight, and climbed into the small room. Making his way over to the attic window, he rubbed enough dirt off to let a ray of sunshine in. He recognized a child's wooden rocker shaped like a horse. He smiled. *Oh, how I loved my Rocky. I rode that thing all over the house. Mom got mad when I fell off the porch with it.*

As he looked around, he found four cardboard boxes stacked in a corner with no labels. He slowly carried each one down to the living room so he could inspect the contents. Plus, he wasn't sure what he would find. *If there's a snake inside, I want some room to get away or kill it,* he thought.

After setting the boxes in front of the faded green couch, he slapped the cushion hard, creating a billowing cloud of rising dust. He didn't care about the dirt; he cared if he was bitten by a critter hidden under or between the cushions. *It would be embarrassing to be bitten on the butt and try to explain that at the ER.*

Slowly sitting down, he used his Case knife to open the first box.

To his surprise, it was filled with *Southern Living* magazines. He knew his mother enjoyed the magazine and was always excited to get one each month. *Mom loved to try all those new recipes on Daddy and me.* Joe laughed. Looking closer, he saw the top magazine was the very first edition, number one, dated February 1966. *That might be worth some money nowadays. Might need to keep this box.*

Joe opened the second box expecting a big surprise, but he only found old clothes. The third box was just as disappointing. It contained several books...the covers torn, the pages stained and tattered. He dragged the last box in front of him and yanked the tape off, thinking he was really wasting his time.

His jaw dropped. He gasped. He didn't expect the treasures his eyes beheld. He clutched a small clear case in his hand. What was inside brought a tear. *Daddy's dog tags. Oh, Daddy! I will never let them out of my sight!* Next, he picked up an old photo—his parents' wedding picture. Faded and creased, he traced his fingers over the picture as if to hug them. There were several family photos, many of whom Joe had no clue who they were. *All these people in these black and whites are no doubt dead. The clothes they are wearing prove that for sure.* His hands trembled as he lifted his mother's Bible to his chest. It was as if he felt her presence beside him.

At the bottom of the box was a small stack of letters. Immediately, Joe recognized the name and return address on each letter. As he untied a thin red ribbon wrapped around the collection, he thumbed through the envelopes. All but one of the letters were to Joe Asher during his tour in Desert Storm. The first letter was addressed to Any Service Member. He smiled and thought, *I've never forgotten her.*

As if the past had caught up to the present, he ran his fingers over her written name. He carefully laid the letters aside. He fought the urge to open and read. *If I read one, I'll read all of them and I'll end up here all night. It's getting late in the day. I'll wait 'til I get home. Damn it, I think I need a drink.* He loaded up his truck with all the family memories. He placed the letters in the front seat. *I wonder what she is doing now. It's been such a long time ago,* he said to himself.

The bumps and potholes didn't stop Joe from driving quickly out of the holler. He wanted to get back to his house in Norton, kick back with a whiskey, and take a minute for his thoughts to leave the past and return to the present day. He knew he was doing the right thing, to tear down the old homeplace. It was unlivable and to repair it would cost as much as a new house. He wasn't sure if he would re-build or just sell the property. His age factored into all his decisions. *I don't want to be the crazy old man who lived in the holler.*

By the time Joe settled into his recliner, it was dusky dark. He be-gan to reflect. Without hesitation, he took a big swallow of his Jack Daniels and read the first letter from a woman named Lucy, who later racked his brain and stole his heart. It was a pleasant letter, not unlike several he received during that time. Yet, her letters quickly became very important to him.

In 1991, Lucy Hale was an Emergency Room nurse, working in a hospital in Corbin, Kentucky. She was divorced with one daughter. Joe, a young marine, felt an urge to respond to her letter...and he did. Even through the conflict, the lack of sleep, and the miserable conditions of war, Joe kept in touch. It was a feeling, a connection.

When Joe's tour ended, the letters stopped. He chose to leave the military and return home to care for his elderly parents in Asher Holler. His love for the simple mountain life overshadowed any idea of living anywhere else. He worked in construction until he bought a small trucking company which he maintained until he retired. In addition, he had kept up with an ongoing relationship with a woman in Virginia he had met a few years earlier. He enjoyed Sally's company during their courtship. Yet, at times he felt insignificant when he was in the midst of her relatives. Marriage had been the next logical step, or so he thought.

A loud clap of thunder caused Joe to wake from a deep sleep. He was still holding Lucy's last letter in his hand. *I wonder if she is still in Corbin. She's probably married with five kids and ten grandkids by now. Still, I think I will write her a note just in case. Who knows!* He grabbed a piece of notebook paper and finally found a pen. He stared at the blank sheet of paper, not really knowing how to start. Getting frustrated, he rambled a few sentences, tore it up, and eventually became satisfied with his message.

*Dear Lucy,*

*I realize far too much time has passed since our words crossed the waters, but I just want you to know I still have all your letters. If you have any free time, I would like to thank you in person, perhaps over a cup of coffee. Please let me know when and where.*

*Your Friend,*
*Joe Asher*

He knew the odds weren't in his favor that Lucy would receive the letter. *She probably doesn't even live in Kentucky now, but I gotta try.* Early the next morning, he dropped it in the outgoing mailbox at the post office. Then he returned to Asher Holler to meet with the company he hired to demolish the house and clean up the area. His emotions ran high as he drove up the dirt road. It was a hard decision, but he felt it was the right one. He couldn't keep the house in such bad disrepair. He accepted the fact that he was too old to try to restore it to become livable. He felt that his parents would agree with him.

After going over the contract one more time with a local construction company, Joe was satisfied with the price and the promise that all the work would be completed within a couple of months unless there was bad weather. He looked one last time at the place he called home, remembering the good times and bad. With a tear in his eye and a sad smile on his lips, he dropped his head as he climbed back into his truck for the ride back to Virginia.

Several weeks had passed when he received the letter he had been hoping for. Quickly tearing open the envelope, he read her words once again. He learned Lucy still resided in Corbin. She retired a few years ago from being a Physician's Assistant and continued to enjoy the single life. Her son and his family lived nearby along with two grandsons who were attending college.

At the end of her letter, she wrote that she would be happy to join him for a cup of coffee. She provided her phone number, asking Joe to call her when he had some free time. *Oh, I've got free time! I've got plenty of time!* That afternoon he dialed her number. His hand trembled.

After three rings, Lucy answered. "Hello."

Joe took a breath. "Lucy, this is Joe Asher. Just wanted to thank you for answering my letter. I know it's been a long time and I hoped you still had the same address."

"I was really shocked, to say the least. I've never forgotten our letters. If you're coming up this way any time soon, I would like to buy you that cup of coffee," Lucy offered.

"Sounds fine to me. Anytime is good. Just let me know when and where?"

"How about Thursday, the day after tomorrow, that is if you are free? Let's meet in the afternoon at the Depot on Main Street. How about two p.m.?"

"It's a date. I'll see you on Thursday."

"This is such a nice surprise after all these years. See you soon."

After they hung up, panic set in. Joe felt the urge to back out, to cancel. *I don't know if I'm getting into something I don't need. Maybe I ought to just forget it. No, I can't do that. I'll go and if I've made a mistake, so be it. I'll make up an excuse and leave early. It's not like a couple of hours is gonna change my life anyway.*

In the blink of an eye, it was Thursday morning. Joe wrestled with thoughts of going early and sitting in the truck until he saw her. He had kept a small picture of Lucy in his wallet all these years, a young Lucy. Would he even recognize the woman who gave him so much hope during a time of war?

The trip from Norton to Corbin was a pleasant one. With the crisp autumn breeze and the beauty of the colorful mountains, his nerves settled down as he drove over the winding roads. Living in the mountain area most of his life, Joe was familiar with the town of Corbin and surrounding areas. He found a parking space nearly in front of the restaurant. Being a few minutes early, he stayed inside the truck, watching for his pen pal to arrive.

Joe recognized her as soon as she crossed the street in front of the Depot. He didn't understand why he felt so anxious...so excited yet terrified. He quickly got out of the truck, meeting her as she came to the restaurant's entrance.

He smiled. "Hello, Lucy."

"Joe! It's so good to finally meet you after all these years." She smiled.

"Let's not stand here. Let's go in and get a table." Joe opened the door for her.

There was no lack of conversation between the two people who, somehow, had created a special bond decades ago. They both felt free to talk about their past and the present. Joe was relieved when Lucy told him that she wasn't involved with anyone. Lucy seemed equally happy to hear he didn't have a special lady in his life. Both were cautious with their questions but quite satisfied with the answers.

Two hours passed quickly. During the lengthy conversations, Joe told Lucy about the old homeplace and his decision to reluctantly let it go. Lucy was very intrigued and accepted his invitation to see the house before it was demolished. They made a date for Saturday. She decided it was much easier to meet him at his residence in Norton than to try to find Asher Holler.

After leaving the Depot, Joe walked Lucy to her car. She turned to him. She started to say something. Joe cupped her face, leaned down, and kissed her forehead. It was the most romantic gesture Lucy had ever felt. Joe looked into her beautiful blue eyes. No words were spoken. Time stopped if only for that moment. It was a simple expression that brought this man and woman an unexpected tenderness.

Joe watched as Lucy drove away. He returned to his truck and sped back to Norton. He surprised himself with the feelings he showed. *I can't believe I did that. I wonder what she thought.* He talked to himself all the way back home. That night he was restless, his mind still racing. After several hours of tossing and turning in the bed, he finally got up around four a.m. and made a huge breakfast of biscuits and gravy.

The rest of the day, Joe raked the leaves in the yard, filling up three large garbage bags. He cleaned his truck and sprayed the small driveway. Inside his house, he vacuumed, dusted, and washed the few dishes in the kitchen sink. He looked to keep himself busy. For the first time in a very long time, he whistled a happy tune. That night as he readied for bed, he took his wedding ring off.

On Saturday morning, Lucy pulled into Joe's driveway. He greeted her at the door. "Come on in. Did you have any trouble finding the place?"

"No, it was a really nice drive. I hope I'm not too early."

"No, you are just fine. I've been up for hours. Come have a seat in the living room. Would you like a bottle of water or some sweet tea?"

"I'd love a sweet tea if it's not too much trouble," Lucy said. "You have a very nice home here."

"Thank you." Joe returned from the kitchen with a tall glass of sweet tea. "There's no reason for you to follow me to the holler so let's just take my truck and leave your car parked here, if that's okay with you?"

Lucy agreed.

After a short conversation, they decided it was time to get on the road to Asher Holler. Joe was somewhat nervous, and he could tell that Lucy seemed to be the same way. There had been intimate feelings with that kiss on her forehead that neither of them expected.

The trip was quick. Both made an effort to avoid a long silence. As Joe parked the vehicle, Lucy's attention was on the large old house within walking distance. Surrounded by the multitude of colorful autumn trees, the house captured a scene of beauty.

"God paints a purty picture in these hollers. Joe, are you sure you want to get rid of your homeplace after all these years? I mean, it carries so many memories for you."

"The company I hired will be here this week to take it down. I told them they could gut the inside first and keep whatever they want. I was here earlier and got all I wanted. That is when I found your letters that my mother had kept in the attic for me. I didn't even know."

"Just be sure this is what you want," Lucy said. "There's no rush."

Joe gently reached over and held her hand. "I think you are right."

Lucy looked up at Joe. "Sometimes something unexpected happens that's meant to stay in your life and bring you joy. You just got to watch for them."

"I think I am looking at one right here with me," he said, as he took her into his arms.

All his fears and doubts disappeared. He felt her passion, her warmth, the love he had longed for. Their kiss sealed their future, knowing that after all these years they were meant to be together... and they were.

# The Face of Her Dreams

## Linda Hudson Hoagland

Every night Ellen would lie awake thinking about what she had dreamed. Why was she replaying the same scene over and over again?

The face she saw in her dreams was unknown to her. She had never met anyone who even resembled the perfectly featured, sleeping man who peered at her from between the ivy leaves she saw every night. She never got to hear his voice or know anything about him except that he appeared to be a statue, or merely a mask, created in the fashion of the Greeks and Romans in past centuries, and he was infiltrating her dreams each and every night.

His face was beautiful but unmoving, so perfect and unblemished with marks of anxiety, fear, or possibly even age.

Why were his eyes always closed? Why was he always peering at her as if from a permanent sleep? Why was he looking through the green tendrils of ivy as if his face was being covered by the growing vegetation that was trying to obscure his astounding good looks? Was he peering at her from between the branches of the foliage of bushes and trees or was he watching her from the ground as the brown earth and vegetation tried to absorb his body?

Ellen was getting to the point of being excited about going to bed and going to sleep. Her mind was filled with thoughts of dreaming of his return, but the excitement was becoming tinged with dread for reasons unknown to her.

* * *

"Why do people dream?" she asked her coworker, Sandy, one day.

"Your mind always dreams. You just don't remember them all the time."

"What about having the same dream over and over again?"

"You mean a nightmare?" Sandy questioned.

"No, not really, just the same story or the same person in the dream each and every time. Actually, it's the only dream I can remember at all."

"I'd call that a nightmare," said Sandy.

"I wouldn't."

"Maybe it's a warning."

Ellen considered the possibility. "What kind of warning?"

"What's the dream about?" asked Sandy as she tried to make sense of Ellen's problem.

"I dream of this good-looking man. He appears in my dreams and then he fades away."

"How does he fade away? Does he die? Leave town? Or what?"

"I don't know. He's just gone."

"I don't know what to tell you, Ellen. It really sounds more like a nightmare to me. It sounds like the warning of death."

"No, I don't think that is what it is at all. Thanks anyway, Sandy. Maybe I'll find out what it means sooner or later. I don't think it's a bad thing."

\* \* \*

Ellen's dreams continued, but the visits from the beautiful, sleeping face were becoming shorter and shorter in duration. She seemed to be getting only fleeting glimpses of his green-hued face peering from the ever-expanding, ever-growing tendrils of ivy as it reached across him to hide his beauty from the world.

\* \* \*

After several more nights of passing glances in her sleep, Ellen decided to spend an evening with her friend Bertha at the bar for drinks. Ellen was not outgoing like her friend, so she tended to shrink into the background away from the crowd while Bertha enjoyed the spotlight.

She sipped on her drink and observed the people around her. Then, suddenly, she saw him—the face of her dreams. The resemblance was amazing. The youthfulness and the perfectly chiseled features were displayed warmly on the man's smiling face as he approached her.

"Hi, my name is Jack," he said as he bowed in front of her.

"I'm Ellen."

"Have we met before?"

"Only in my dreams," whispered Ellen as she rose to dance with Jack after he extended his arm in invitation.

Jack held her close, and Ellen felt the thrill of excitement travel up and down her spine. She felt as if she had known Jack forever and that it was natural for her to follow his lead wherever he might want to take her. She was in love with Jack, the man whom she had just met and who was guiding her over the dance floor as if that were his only purpose in life.

Ellen knew she was in love with her dream face, not Jack, but she couldn't tell her body not to respond to his touch. She couldn't stop the adrenaline rush and the tingling of her spine that made her feel like she was floating on air. She couldn't control the pounding of her heart as it forced blood into the areas deep in her body that yearned for his tender touch. The yearning was an excruciatingly wonderful pain that opened her up like a blossom reaching full bloom.

"Let's get out of here," Jack whispered.

Ellen didn't answer. She grabbed her handbag and tucked her arm around his.

"Do you have a car?"

"Over there," said Ellen as she pointed down the street.

"Give me your key."

Jack unlocked the door and helped Ellen into the passenger seat. He walked around the car and climbed in behind the steering wheel.

"Where to?"

Ellen gave him her address.

Upon arriving at her house, Ellen led Jack up the stairs to her bedroom. Few words were spoken between the two destined lovers. No words were needed. Only the actions and feelings of love were necessary to bind them together into one.

Jack made soft, gentle love to Ellen, coaxing her to experience sensations and feelings she had only dreamed of after reading about them in books.

Ellen made love to Jack in return. She allowed no part of his body to escape the touch of her lips or the sweet caress of her searching tongue.

When Ellen had finished loving Jack, she watched him as he fell into quiet slumber beside her. She propped herself up on her elbow and traced his face with her fingertips accentuating each and every feature that she had envisioned in her dreams so often at night. She followed the line of his jawbone to his neck and onto his chest which was lightly sprinkled with the curly hair of manhood. His body was not that of a Greek or Roman god because it led to a slight swell of a tummy that had indulged in too much beer. She traced his short, stocky legs down to his feet where he moved his foot slightly from her tickling touch.

Ellen smiled at the manly beauty stretched in front of her. "You may not be a Greek or Roman god, but you are my man, and I don't ever want to let you go," she whispered with a smile of determination as she fell back onto the bed beside him.

Ellen slipped into an exhausted but blissful sleep only to wake up and find that she was alone. The scents of sweet sex lingered in the air and the imprints of his beautiful body on the cotton sheets were the only reminders of her visitor.

The warm, sweet, sated smile plastered on her face was not going to be removed for days.

* * *

Ellen went back to the same bar almost every night for several months looking for Jack.

"Have you seen Jack?" she asked everyone she met.

"Jack who?"

"I don't know his last name. He has dark blond hair, blue eyes, and a wonderful smile."

"I'm sorry. I don't know him," was the usual response.

45

She knew he would come back. He had to come back. There was nothing else that he could do. That's why she returned to that bar every night herself; there was nothing else that she could do.

"What will it be?" asked the bartender as he wiped the old, scarred, wooden bar top in front of Ellen.

"Rum and Coke, bottled Coke, please."

"I'm new around here," the bartender told her. "My name is Harold. What's yours?"

"Ellen."

"May I buy you a drink, Ellen?"

"Does it obligate me to anything?" She scrutinized Harold's face.

"What?"

"I mean, if you buy me a drink or more than one drink, will I have to repay the debt by sleeping with you?"

Harold's mouth dropped open as his mind searched for words to respond. Finally, he said, "No, no strings attached at all."

Ellen realized she shouldn't have said out loud what she had been thinking. "I'm sorry. I didn't mean for you to hear that. My answer should have been a polite 'no.'"

"You've had some problems in the past, I take it."

"Yes, I have. I usually decline drinks without any kind of explanation except that I'm waiting for someone."

"You've been here several nights in a row. I saw you every night that I was checking this place out before I started working here. I've never seen you with anyone. Who are you waiting for?"

"His name is Jack. He has dark blond hair, blue sparkling eyes, and a warm engaging smile that spreads across his entire face. Have you seen him?" Ellen's voice was hopeful.

"I can't say that I have but, then again, I'm new around here."

"Thanks anyway," she sighed.

"Do you still want that 'no strings attached' drink?" He smiled kindly at her.

"Sure. I'd like that. Thank you."

* * *

Ellen continued her search, frequenting the bar every night until one day she found a heavy-set young man with sad eyes, whom she was certain she had seen the night she met Jack.

"Have you seen Jack?" she asked happily as she scooted over a couple of barstools to sit next to the young man.

He turned his head to look at Ellen with eyes that held no sign of happiness. "No, Jack's dead," he responded softly.

"What?" Ellen felt like she'd just been slapped.

"He was mugged on his way home from a lady's house in Lakewood a few months ago when he was jumped by a couple of thugs. They robbed him and killed him."

"Oh, I'm so sorry," said Ellen as the tears started to fall down her cheeks.

"Did you know him well?" asked the young man.

"I'm the lady from Lakewood...and I loved him. He was the face of my dreams."

# Whisper at Katbird Creek

*Jan Howery*

Kate sat in the homemade, braided rope swing that dangled from the tall oak tree's strongest limb, which shaded the edge of a small, gently flowing creek. The swing had been placed there by her dad when she was six years old. You could not see the swing or the creek from their 1860's farmhouse, but it was an easy walk down a dirt path, and it was a peaceful, hidden getaway. The barn was built near the creek for the horses and cows so that they both could graze near the creek.

Kate gently swayed back and forth on the swing. Her thoughts went to her sixteenth birthday, which was in September. It was on her birthday, in late afternoon, that she secretly met the love of her life, Lamarie Duke. She recalled how Lamarie rode his derby-winning horse, Fire, and blazed through the edge of the woods to meet her at the old oak tree.

Lamarie eased out of the saddle, dismounted the horse, and draped the horse's reins over a small bush. He walked slowly over to Kate, and clasped her hands in his hands, looked into her eyes, and said, "You are so beautiful." He gently kissed her on the lips.

"When can I ask your father for your hand in marriage?" he asked and whispered in her ear. "We've been sneaking around now for six months. I want to marry you. You are now sixteen years old and old enough to marry."

"Lamarie, my father will never approve of a marriage between us," Kate said tearfully. "I...I think we should stop seeing each other."

"You can't mean that. I love you and I know that you love me," Lamarie said softly.

Lamarie's family was not financially equal to Kate's family. Kate's dad was a successful dairy farmer and was well respected in the community. Lamarie's dad had passed away when he was ten years old, and his mother and four siblings struggled to make ends meet. Lamarie, now twenty-one, was a hard worker, and because of his love of horses, he had been successful in taking an unknown thoroughbred and winning several horse races with large cash awards.

"Let's just sneak away and get married," Lamarie said sweetly. He kissed Kate passionately and pulled her body next to his. Desire engulfed Kate's entire body. She yearned for him. They both gently fell to the ground, and under the oak tree, they made love for the first time.

They declared their love for each other that afternoon and decided to meet there at the oak tree in a couple of days to run away.

As planned, Kate showed up at the oak tree, prepared to run away with Lamarie. She waited. It was late afternoon, and the air was very cold. Time passed. The daylight was washed away by the darkness. She patiently sat on the swing, but Lamarie never showed. She felt a chill that penetrated to her bones. Tears filled her eyes.

"Kate! Are you out here?" a voice rang out loudly from around the barn.

She recognized the voice. "Yes, Daddy, I'm here," Kate said sadly.

"What on earth are you doing out here? It's dark and the air is freezing. You need to get back to the house. I put the horses in the barn tonight 'cause it's going to be so frigid," her dad said.

Kate stood up from the swing and looked toward the woods. There, in the distance, she saw Lamarie standing beside his horse, and he began walking toward her. Kate turned to her dad and quickly looked back at Lamarie, but he was gone. She hesitated.

Kate's dad said, "Come on. And I need to tell you something that I heard in town today."

He grabbed her arm. Kate reluctantly walked along with him.

"I heard some news in town today," he continued. "I heard that Lamarie boy, who you're so crazy about...well...he was racing that race-horse of his, and the horse fell, throwing him off...and the horse... well...it just fell right on 'em, and Lamarie died right there."

Kate gasped. Her knees went weak. She stumbled to the ground.

"I know it's dark, but watch your step," her dad instructed and grabbed her arm.

She stood and glanced back to the edge of the woods and trees. Even in the darkness, she saw Lamarie standing there. She knew it was untrue. She pulled away from her dad and looked at Lamarie.

"Where on earth are you doing? Come on now. It's dark. And there's nothing following us. We need to get back to the house," Kate's dad said and wrapped his arm around her waist to pull her along. She tried to look back as they walked back to the house, but she saw nothing but darkness.

The news spread fast that Lamarie had died. Kate was devastated.

For months, each day, Kate walked down the dirt path to the oak tree, sat in her swing, and hoped to see Lamarie. She believed that La-marie was alive and would come back for her. He promised. She had seen him. But Lamaire never showed.

\* \* \*

The days turned into months, and soon everyone was decorating for the Christmas holiday.

On Christmas Eve night, the weather was frigid. It was a cold, snowy night. But even with an arctic coldness, Kate had a plan. She waited until everyone was in bed, and at midnight, she quietly tiptoed out the door and walked down the dirt path to the oak tree.

*Tonight, Lamarie will come for me*, she thought. *He will come for me. He promised.*

She sat down on her swing. She gently swayed back and forth. The full moon peeked through the clouds as they swirled around in the sky. The full moon was shining so brightly that Katie could see the frigid water trinkle over the small rocks in the creek. She watched the cascading water, and it was as if the creek whispered to her: "He's coming for you. He's coming for you tonight."

Hours passed, and snowflakes began to gently fall again. The temperature kept dropping. Kate patiently waited for Lamarie to come and get her.

Just as Kate was about to succumb to the cold temperature, a whisper broke the silence of the night. She recognized the whisper.

"I love you."

Kate jumped up and turned around, and there stood Lamarie smiling and holding his horse's rein in his hand. He extended his other hand out to her and sweetly whispered, "I've come for you. I promised."

She smiled and took his hand. Together, they mounted his horse, Fire, and disappeared into the woods.

\* \* \*

51

On Christmas morning, while making his early morning feedings to the horses and cows at the barn, Kate's dad was shocked to see Kate sitting on the swing. He quickly ran over to her, only to find her frozen body sitting upright on the swing.

"Kate! Kate!"

Kate didn't respond. He was devastated.

"Why? Why? Why?" he yelled. He tried to remove her from the swing, but her tiny fingers were frozen holding onto the rope.

Kate's dad slowly and meticulously cut the swing's ropes and lowered it to the ground. He carried Kate and the swing to the farmhouse.

At the funeral, the swing was placed inside Kate's coffin with her.

### Five Years Later

"Hey, look at that swing. Let's go play at that old oak tree!"

Three of the neighbor's children ran toward the swing. As they approached it, they stopped in their tracks when a young girl suddenly appeared sitting on the swing. She smiled and whispered sweetly to them, "Not today. This is my swing."

The swing disappeared as a young girl, a young man, and a spirited horse disappeared into the dark woods.

Legend has it, when there's a full moon on Christmas Eve, you can hear whispers at Katbird Creek.

# Extra Security

*Draco Sage*

### LACHLAN

The metal clang of the stairwell door was too loud through the computer speakers. Lachlan nearly dropped the book he'd been reading as he flipped his wrist to check the time.

"4:30 already?" he asked the empty control room. But his watch read just 3 p.m. Lachlan closed his novel and pulled his chair up to the desk. He gazed at monitor six. Darcy, the usually perky jewelry counter clerk, was pacing back and forth on the stair landing. Lachlan squinted at the screen as Darcy went from wringing his hands one moment to haphazardly running them through his hair the next. Then he heard a sob. Darcy leaned back against the wall and dropped his head into his hands. Lachlan watched in turmoil as the man on the screen let himself weep. Shuddering breaths and snot-filled sniffs permeated the silence.

Lachlan pushed to his feet but couldn't bring himself to move further. After all, what was he to say? He and Darcy had met various times, sure. They'd shared small talk and heavy passing glances, flirted at company parties, and spent time in the same spaces through mutual friends, but he couldn't exactly say, 'I wait until 4:30 p.m. every day just to watch you take your break in the stairwell because seeing you takes my breath away.'

"God, it sounds like I belong on a list or something!" He grimaced. Darcy was still there. It was 3:04 now. Company breaks were fifteen minutes long. He wanted to be there for him, to say something that would make Darcy laugh or smile, offer a tissue, reassurance, and a reminder that none of the bullshit that happens in this dumb department store actually matters. But Lachlan knew that if he showed up now there would be no way to play it off as coincidence. Darcy knew he worked security; he'd know Lachlan had been spying on him in his moment of upset.

Lachlan sat back down on the edge of his seat with a huff. *Maybe I should switch that camera off instead to give him some privacy.* His fingers hovered over the keyboard as he chewed on his bottom lip. Then, just as he was about to commit, Darcy shoved off from the wall and started barreling down the steps. Lachlan followed his movements frantically from screen to screen as he was picked up by one camera after the next until he landed on the ground floor and exited into the alleyway. The view from the alley camera caught Darcy resting once more against the wall, just barely in view. He wiped his cheeks and leaned his head back in what Lachlan could only assume was a desperately needed deep breath.

*Screw it.* Lachlan dashed out the door of the control room. He checked his watch again—3:07. Just two floors above the ground, Lachlan made it down the stairwell in record time. He lingered inside to catch his breath, lest he look as crazy as he felt having just chased his crush down several flights of stairs. *Ugh, crush. What am I, twelve?* Sometimes Darcy made him feel twelve. That is to say, Darcy spurred an excitement in Lachlan that seemed lost at other times, a feeling akin only to childlike wonder and the same hummingbird wing heartbeat that comes from a first love.

After a deep breath of his own, Lachlan pushed open the door and peeked around. There stood Darcy, eyes closed and pinching the bridge of his nose between his thumb and finger. The chilled air had already painted a pink tint on his cheeks despite having only been outside a brief time. Lachlan now noticed that it was sprinkling rain. Each drop that clung to Darcy's brunette locks made his hair seem to sparkle in the afternoon sun as it dipped in and out from behind greying clouds. Even in dismay, Darcy was stunning. He had a jawline as sharp as his wit and sandy skin that Lachlan could only imagine evoked the same feeling as curling your toes in sun-kissed beaches. He let the door close softly.

Darcy startled at the sound. "Oh sorry," he began and stepped toward the door, but upon recognition paused again. "Lachlan," he breathed. "Hey."

Misty, amber eyes met his own and Lachlan knew he was fucked. He'd had every intention of playing the whole situation off—'Oh, I'm just on break, you too? Funny coincidence.' But suddenly lying to Darcy seemed like a capital offense. He slipped off his security jacket and held it out. In just a thin, long-sleeved Henley, Darcy was shivering. "It's cold out here, you know?"

"Thanks..." Darcy nodded as he donned the garment, giving Lachlan an elegant view of the long, smooth lines of his form in motion. There was a pregnant silence between them until Darcy blurted, "I wasn't trying to get your attention. I should've gone off to the bathroom or something, I just needed a moment uninterrupted—"

"Do you want me to leave?"

"No!" Suddenly the cold wasn't the only thing causing Darcy's cheeks to flame. He glanced away in embarrassment before more calmly repeating, "No, I didn't mean it like that. I just meant that it wasn't my intention to cause a disturbance. I'm sure I put on a pitiful show for the cameras."

"Eh, it wasn't party-worthy or anything," Lachlan mused. He mimicked Darcy's lean against the concrete exterior and glanced over at him.

Darcy feigned an exaggerated chuckle. "Very funny, *Paul Blart*."

A smirk played on Lachlan's lips. "All right, I deserved that." Darcy, whose chin fell in line with Lachlan's shoulder, squinted up at him. He could see the dampness of both tears and rain on lightly freckled cheeks. "Do you want to talk about it?"

Darcy shrugged. "Just retail crap, you know? Between shit managers and shit customers, we're treated like servants. Sometimes people say things that really get to me."

"What got to you today?" Lachlan encouraged him to continue.

Darcy produced a rather stately brooch from the pocket of his slacks. The golden rim was dotted with peach gemstones that glinted as he passed the ornate jewelry into the security guard's palm. Lachlan held the piece up to study its center. A carved image, presumably of shell or bone, depicted two men locked in an embrace, the tips of their noses just barely touching.

"Wow," Lachlan whispered. "This is...beautiful." He glanced back to Darcy as he spoke, hoping the multitudes of his meaning could be felt. The flutter of eyelashes and soft smile that responded told him that it was.

"Thank you. It was a gift." Darcy pointed to the brooch's edge. "The outer frame is vintage. Those are pink sapphires. It once held a different centerpiece, years ago when it belonged to my grandmother. But somehow it broke, and the original center was lost over time."

Lachlan watched Darcy's face change as he recounted the story. The frustration and sadness from before began to melt away and in its place came a peaceful warmth.

"After I came out," Darcy went on, "My grandmother had a new centerpiece handmade for me. She gave it to me as a way to show her support." His fingers brushed against Lachlan's skin as he picked up the brooch and pocketed it once again. "It always made her smile to see me wear it." He sighed. "And then today...some bigot asked to see it and I foolishly showed it to her. She made a fucking complaint right then and there to Patrick, and instead of backing me up, the bastard told me not to wear it! He sat there and listened to her call me every slur she could think of and did absolutely nothing."

A sickening fury began bubbling in Lachlan's stomach. Darcy sounded so defeated. It was a feeling Lachlan knew all too well, that of fighting to just exist in the same ways and spaces as everyone else without being subject to disgusting glances and even more disgusting behavior.

"Can I hug you?" he whispered.

Darcy huffed a half-hearted chuckle. "Yes please."

It wasn't the first time they'd embraced, having shared other short, sideways hugs in greeting at sporadic gatherings or in group photos here and there. But it was the first time Lachlan truly got to hold him. It was the first time he felt Darcy bury his nose in the crook of his neck. The first time he felt a thundering against his chest and couldn't tell if it came from Darcy's heart or his own. He breathed in the scent of vanilla cologne and hoped it would linger in his nostrils forever.

"I'm sorry it's been such a shit day," Lachlan whispered.

"Has it? Suddenly I seem to have forgotten all about it." He felt Darcy's lips tremble against his skin as he spoke.

"Glad I could help."

The buzz of Darcy's phone startled them both. Lachlan reluctantly released him. He checked his watch. *Damn.* It was 3:25.

"Ugh, I'm late."

Lachlan knew Darcy was right, but he shrugged anyway. "Screw 'em. I think you earned a few extra minutes."

"Somehow I don't think Patrick will agree." The jewelry clerk rolled his eyes. He was already rushing for the door. Lachlan caught the handle and held it open before following Darcy inside. They hurried up the stairs, the sound of their boots echoing off the walls. Lachlan followed Darcy all the way up to the fourth floor, merely grinning when they passed the second story entrance, and his companion shot him a questioning look.

When they reached the fourth landing, he grasped the door again but before opening it said, "You know where to find me if you need me. It's literally my job to throw bitches out."

Darcy laid his hand on Lachlan's muscled bicep and grinned. "Yeah, you look like you could throw somebody around."

Dumbfounded, Lachlan couldn't come up with a single thing to respond. He held the door open in tongue-tied silence and watched as Darcy winked at him, put on a brave countenance, and marched back onto the floor. *Cheeky bastard.* A giddy expression plastered itself across his face, remaining there the whole walk back to the security control room. He collapsed in his chair, exhilarated in almost the same way many of his interactions with Darcy made him feel. *But like, tripled.*

Lachlan stared at the monitors on the desk without really seeing them and shook his head gently to clear his mind and, hopefully, the flush creeping up his neck and face. He felt a short vibration in his pocket.

A text from an unsaved number read: Thanks by the way. I really do feel much better.

Lachlan typed a quick reply: Sorry, who is this?

How many damsels in distress have you rescued today?

Hang on, let me think...

I'll wait.

Lachlan busied himself setting up Darcy's contact, not bothering to ask where the man had gotten his number in the first place. He left his reply unsent for a minute or two, just to tease a little anticipation.

Darcy, however, was not to be kept waiting: Well detective?

Lachlan chuckled. Just one damsel today. Kind of a slow day for me.

There was no response this time, and Lachlan saw on monitor four that the jewelry counter was getting busy. Darcy traipsed in and out of view helping customers. As he watched the retail havoc, a realization came over him. He leaned forward on the desk and began clicking through the last several hours of recorded footage from the jewelry counter, pausing each time Patrick was on the screen. He switched the volume on. After a few minutes of searching, a shout came through the speakers. Lachlan allowed the recording to play, and the more he listened, the angrier he became.

It was a scene just as Darcy had described. A middle-aged woman smacked her hand on the jewelry counter. She gestured angrily at Darcy, but only addressed Patrick as if speaking to Darcy was beneath her. In response to every disgusting utterance, the manager placated her, until finally Lachlan heard him instruct Darcy to take his grandmother's brooch off and assured the wretch not to worry, that he'd make sure the jewelry clerk didn't wear it again.

Lachlan had heard enough. He picked up his phone and dialed a number he'd honestly had to call too often at this damn job. As it rang, he rewound the recording and made a separate clip of the scene.

A voice as sweet as honey answered his call. "Human Resources Department, how may I help you?"

"Charlie? It's Lachlan. I have an issue I need to report."

"Hey, Lach! Are we adding another one to the banned customer list?" He heard her nails on her keyboard as she began a new complaint file.

"I wish. I don't know the customer's name, unfortunately. I'm actually calling to report the manager involved."

There was a beat of silence. "Is it Patrick?"

Lachlan smirked. *Karma's a bitch, my guy.* "Had complaints about him before, I'm guessing?"

"A couple. What is it this time?"

He explained the situation in as much detail as he could without including his personal interest or Darcy's family affairs. Then, he sent Charlie a quick email with the recording. He heard her open it in the background and tsk as Patrick showed his ass.

"Three strikes and you're out, Pat," Charlie muttered. "We'll get it taken care of, Lachlan, thanks for letting me know."

"No problem. Have a good one, Charlie."

Lachlan set his phone aside and picked up the book he'd been reading. Now and then, he checked on monitor four and occasionally caught Darcy peeking up at the camera himself.

He sent a quick message after the first time or two. Aren't you supposed to be working?

The reply was instant. Aren't you?

Lachlan leaned back in his chair and stared up at the ceiling, his heart rate feeling like it was approaching dangerous levels. "This guy is going to be the death of me," he groaned. *If only I should be so lucky.*

## DARCY

Darcy glanced around the jewelry counter in dismay. It was a bit of a mess after the busyness of the night before. A stack of small, empty boxes was scattered across the glass, there was just one gift bag left in supply, and the entire case was covered in fingerprint smudges. He heaved a sigh and checked the time. It was 8 a.m. He had an hour until the store opened.

Darcy logged into the computer and pulled up his work email, expecting the usual nonsense about sales numbers, expectations, and food-based bribery practically begging the employees to stick around. It was a favorite pastime of upper management to pretend that this was such a *fun* place to spend one's misery while being paid extraordinarily little and putting up with an incomparable amount of crap. Darcy deleted several meaningless emails without reading them until he came to one for which the subject read 'POLICY REMINDER.' He clicked to open it, ready to read about dress code or breakroom rules yet again. Instead, Darcy was confronted with a policy he'd forgotten the store had.

*A reminder to all employees that we have a zero-tolerance policy for hate speech.*

*Hate speech is considered any conduct that discriminates or incites hatred on the basis of race, religion, sexual or gender identity, ethnicity, or disability. This policy applies to employees AND customers.*

61

*Please click below to read the full policy or view our employee handbook.*

*Sincerely,*
*Upper Management*

Darcy read through the email again. *Weird timing. Maybe someone should tell Patrick.* He scoffed quietly to himself and returned to his inbox. A soft ping signaled a new email at the top of the page.

"Human Resources Department? What the—" The words died in his throat as he began reading.

*Dear Mr. Edwards,*

*It has come to our attention that on the day of February 3, 2023, you were subjected to hate speech-related misconduct at the hands of an immediate manager. We are writing to inform you that the matter has since been rectified.*

*We hope you'll accept our sincerest apologies on behalf of the corporation. Please know that this behavior does not reflect the ideals or policies in our bylaws.*

*Should you have any further complaints, please contact the HR Department.*

*Sincerely,*
*Human Resources Team*

Darcy read and reread the email. "Holy shit..." The clock displayed 8:10—fifty minutes to get the place in order. *Or fifty minutes with Lachlan.* Darcy smirked. *Screw it.* He made his way to the service stairwell, a place that today had a different air about it. With every step down he recalled the way in which his and Lachlan's arms had brushed against one another on their way up yesterday. He breathed in and remembered the scent of Lachlan's cologne—like a fancy rum he wasn't sure he could afford but by god, he was going to pretend he could.

He yanked open the door to the second floor as a smug smile crossed his lips, the image of Lachlan's flummoxed expression when Darcy suggested Lachlan might toss him around burned in his mind. He took considerable pride in making the seemingly fearless security guard feel as sheepish as he did every time they were in the same room. In fact, he quite hoped his cheeky texts yesterday had evoked the same response, though he supposed he'd never know. *Thank god for mutual friends*, he thought, grateful he'd been able to pin down Lachlan's number so quickly.

Light was creeping from underneath the closed door to the control room. Darcy hesitated. *It's now or never.* While that wasn't exactly true, or even true at all, it was enough to get him to knock.

There was a rustling inside as Lachlan rose to answer the intrusion. Darcy's breath caught in his throat as the door swung open. Lachlan grinned at him—goofy and wide and blinding white. The tiniest of gaps peeked out from between his front teeth as his smile pushed his cheeks up to rainforest green eyes that Darcy imagined might cause anyone to lose their way.

"To what do I owe the pleasure?" Lachlan's voice was a soft lullaby Darcy could listen to forever.

He blinked to regain his composure. "Did you get Patrick fired?"

Lachlan laughed, short and humorless. He stepped aside to make room for Darcy to enter. "He got himself fired. All I did was speed things along."

Darcy wasn't sure what to say. After a moment, all he could come up with was, "Why?"

"You deserve to be surrounded by people who respect and support you. And so do all the other people who made complaints about him, but let's be honest, I didn't do it for them."

"You did it for me," Darcy confirmed more to himself than to Lachlan.

But still, Lachlan nodded. "I watch you take your breaks sometimes," he confessed. "Well...almost all of the time."

Darcy raised an eyebrow as Lachlan pointed to one of the monitors on the desk. The screen presented a perfect view of the stair landing where Darcy had spent many a fifteen pacing, lounging, snacking, and escaping from the drudge of his day-to-day.

"You were so dejected...it broke my heart to see you like that. I thought maybe if Patrick got sacked—which he deserved, I might add—I could at least keep him from upsetting you again." Lachlan gently touched his shoulder. "I'm sorry...I shouldn't spy on your breaks. It's creepy as shit and that's not how I want to present myself to you."

Darcy snickered. "It *is* creepy...but now that I know maybe I'll flash you from time to time." Lachlan rolled his eyes and dropped his hand, but not before Darcy felt the slight tremble in his fingertips. "It's just too bad nobody gets to peek in on your breaks too," he pressed.

Lachlan pointed to a camera in the upper corner of the room. He pressed a few buttons on the keyboard until the screen at the end of the desk revealed an image of the two of them standing closer than Darcy realized, their bodies facing one another.

"Hmmm." Darcy pulled his phone from his pocket. He typed a quick message and sent it off only for Lachlan to receive it seconds later.

Will we get fired if I kiss you?

Hand on the mouse, Lachlan kept his face stoic, his eyes never leaving Darcy's as he disabled the control room camera on muscle memory alone.

"Naughty, naughty," Darcy tsked.

Lachlan simpered as he leaned in, shushing Darcy as their lips alighted. Strawberry balm blended with the taste of lemon drop candy in an intoxicating concoction that would've been almost too sweet had it not been exactly what they both needed.

# About the Authors

**Delonda Anderson** is chief editor of the online magazine *Appalachia Bare* and a former editor of *Imaginary Gardens Literary Magazine*. She has a degree in English literature and has published poetry, fiction, and nonfiction. She received a Tennessee Mountain Writers Fiction prize for her short story, "Weep the Wild Cares."

**Karen G. Bruce** is the author of *Josie: A Story of Forgiveness* and *A Heart Never Dies*. Besides writing, Karen is devoted to her two grandchildren and her family's farm in rural Virginia.

**Susan Dickenson** lives in Bristol, Virginia with her husband and two dogs. Dickenson enjoys spending time with her family, birding, and writing. Her short story, "Wisteria Blooms and a Hint of Cotillion," was included in the anthology *Daffodil Dreams*. She is currently working on her debut novel.

A native of Harlan, Kentucky, Appalachian author **Susan Noe Harmon**, has written a novel, *Under the Weeping Willow* and a memoir, *To Hide the Truth*. Currently residing in Florida, her heart remains true to the mountain way of life and its people.

**Linda Hudson Hoagland**, a regional writer from Tazewell, Virginia, has written many mystery novels, along with works of nonfiction, four collections of short writings, and four volumes of poems. Short stories and poems are her favorite pastime, and she has won many awards as well as being published.

**Jan Howery**, a native of Southwest Virginia, writes with an Appalachian influence. Her many writings include "The Daisy Flower Garden," featured in the anthology *Broken Petals*, "Right or Wrong," featured in *Wild Daisies*, "The Love of Daisies" in *Scattered Flowers*, and "Dreams of Being a Teacher" in *Daffodil Dreams*. Her work has also been featured in books one through five of Jan-Carol Publishing's *These Haunted Hills: A Collection of Short Stories* series. Howery's debut novel, *Gone Before Breakfast*, released in 2023, and her second novel is in the works. Other writings include fashion and health columns for the Appalachian regional magazine for women, *Voice Magazine for Women*.

**Draco Sage** resides in Nashville, TN with his fiancé and a home library that boasts around 600 books. He has been published in numerous magazines and anthologies, including Jan-Carol Publishing's *Daffodil Dreams* and *These Haunted Hills Book 5*. When his nose isn't stuck in a novel or notebook, Draco can be found enjoying tabletop RPGs and hosting weekly game nights.

# LOOK FOR OUR OTHER
# SHORT-STORY COLLECTIONS:

# THESE HAUNTED HILLS

A COLLECTION OF SHORT STORIES
BOOK 1, 2, 3, 4, AND 5

**Jan-Carol
Publishing, Inc**

*"every story needs a book"*

**LITTLE CREEK BOOKS
MOUNTAIN GIRL PRESS
EXPRESS EDITIONS
ROSEHEART
BROKEN CROW RIDGE
FIERY NIGHT
SKIPPY CREEK**

**JanCarolPublishing.com**